Spies Go Shopping

Written by Jill Eggleton
Illustrated by Trevor Pye

Rigby

The people in the book

The spy teacher

The spies

The places in the book

The spy teacher looked at the spies.

"You are not spies," she said. "Spies have glasses and coats and hats. Go to the store and get them today!"

So the spies made a list...

and they went shopping.

The spies went into the glasses store.

"Look at all the glasses," they said.

They got pink glasses, blue glasses, green glasses, and orange glasses.

The spies went into
the coat store.
They looked at all the coats.

"Cool coats," they said.

They got purple coats, red coats,
yellow coats, and blue coats.

The spies went into the hat store.

"Cool hats," they said.

They got...

hats with stripes,

hats with spots,

hats with fur,

and hats with feathers.

The spies went back to the spy school.
"Did you get your spy clothes?" said the teacher.
"Yes," said the spies.
"Good," said the teacher. "You can put them on and come with me. You can be spies today."

The spy teacher went
down the road and
the spies went after her.
She went into the park and
the spies went after her.

Park

The kids in the park laughed.

"**Look at the silly spies,**" they said.

The spy teacher looked at the spies.

"You are silly spies," she said. "Go back to the spy school."

ou don’t look like spies,”
said the spy teacher.

“Here is your list…”

Now, get going!
The End
The spies are...
happy?
sad?

Lists

Things for Spies

notebook  Yes? No?

apple  Yes? No?

bag 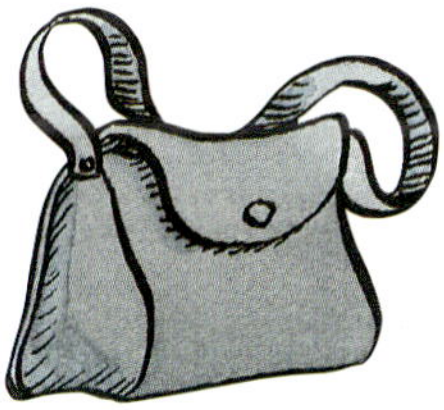 Yes? No?

carrot 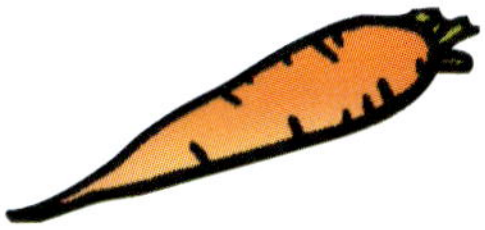 Yes? No?

flashlight 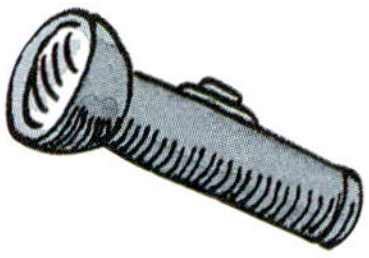 Yes? No?

Word Bank

coat 

feathers 

glasses 

hat 

list 

park 

road 

stores